Charlotte's
Web Page

WESTWOOD SCHOOL
435 SARATOGA AVE.
SANTA CLARA CA. 95050

Contents

Chapter 1

Meet My Folks

Hi there. This is a story about the weirdest half a year of my life. Before I start telling you about it, I suppose I should get all the boring things out of the way. So I'll start with my name. I'm Charlotte Elizabeth Weisner, and I'm going to be twelve in a few weeks, so I feel pretty grown-up and ready to handle whatever life brings.

I live in Boston, which is the Greatest City in the World! Well, my friends and I think it is. We go to Stanley Middle School, which is the Greatest School in Boston, so it makes perfect sense that if Boston is the Greatest City in the World, our school must be the Greatest School in the World.

I also better tell you about my friends, because they are all *mega*important to me. First, there's Claudie. Claudie and I have been in the same class since kindergarten. We balance each other out. Claudie is quiet, and I'm rowdy. If anyone's going to shoot their mouth off, it is going to be me, and while I'm busy making all the noise, Claudie figures out ways to get us out of the trouble I'm getting us into.

Then there is Opu, who draws like nobody I know. She can draw anything. We get her to draw fake tattoos on us with markers. She does awesome dragons and butterflies and stuff like that.

Naiomi is the jock in our group. She plays soccer on weekends. She also runs and does aerobics. Her mother is an instructor at a health club, so I guess it kinda rubs off.

Then there are Brett and Jamie. I know they're boys, but we've always been cool with that, even back when most girls thought boys were diseased creatures. They're part of our group, too, and we all hang out together.

Brett's an encyclopedia of useless information. Sometimes we can be talking about something that happened at school, or something terribly important, such as what movie we should go see, and he'll pipe up with some weird fact that has nothing to do with anything!

And then there is Jamie. Jamie is going to win some competition and get the grand prize of a new car or a trip around the world. You see, he knows where every country is and what people do there. His father works for a travel agency, so Jamie gets

to read all the brochures. You name a place and he'll tell you where it is. He's amazing.

So those are my friends.

I suppose you should also know something about my family. My mom manages the jeans store at the mall. Mom's okay, but she gets very stressed out about everything. She wants to make the shop a success, but it's hard work for her.

Then there is my obnoxious brother, Nathanial. He's three years older than I am. You'd never know from the way he acts. Nat's weird. His friends are weird, too. They are always talking about "What a beauty she is," and it can mean either a car or some girl that just walked by. Get a life!

My brother and his goofy friends go to high school. Sometimes they shut themselves in my brother's bedroom and howl and shriek for hours. But when you burst in on them because you think they're having some great party, all they're doing is staring at my brother's dumb computer screen.

You see, Nat the Nerd is also a computer geek. He spends hours in front of his computer. It's an old one that my dad brought home from work. When Dad gave it to Nat, the nerd acted as excited as I'd be if someone brought me something cool like high heels! This is something I know about because Naiomi, Claudie, and I just bought our first real high-heeled shoes. When my nerdy brother saw my new shoes, he held them up and said, "Hey, nice shoes, stretch! I guess you need some extra height for that basketball career you've been dreaming about."

Of course I said, "Very funny!" and started to chase him around the kitchen. Then Dad put his head in the door and asked, "What's going on?" So I had to say, "Oh, nothing!" and hide my shoes behind my back.

You see, my dad is totally old-fashioned. He wouldn't understand the importance of cool shoes. For that matter, I sometimes think that he doesn't understand people either! He always seems confused by the fact that human beings manage to work without switches and batteries.

Dad is a computer geek, just like Nat. To be more precise, he's called a software engineer, although I think a better job title would be workaholic – I mean, he's *never* at home. He's always late getting home from work, and that's when he's not flying all over the country to fix someone's computer system. He leaves early for work in the morning, too. Most of the time, I just catch sight of him as he's rushing out the door. Sometimes I feel like saying, "Hello. You probably don't remember me, but I'm Charlotte – you know, your daughter?"

It wouldn't make any difference, though. It'd probably be better if I left a message on his computer! He doesn't even see the world around him, let alone me. He has this office in the middle of the city. From his windows you can see right across Boston Harbor. But what does Dad do? He closes his curtains because he says it makes it easier to see his computer screen! All that great view, and he never looks at it! That's what computers do to you.

The other important person in my family is my grandma. She lives down the road from us, and we often go down there on weekends to hang out with her. Right now she is thumping around on crutches because she just had surgery to rebuild her knees, which needed some help after her years of mountain-climbing expeditions with her friends. Yes, Grandma likes extreme sports, and it is always amazing to me that someone as wild and outdoorsy as she is could have ever had a son as nerdy and nonathletic as my dad.

So that's my family for you. Sometimes we have a pretty good time together, but most of the time everyone's always rushing to be somewhere else. Either Mom's all stressed out about the shop, or Dad's about to jump on a plane because some firm's computer system has fallen over and they need Dad to fix it NOW! Or Nat is off to do something geeky. Or I am off to enjoy myself with my friends.

Even Grandma has so many activities and hobbies that, more often than not, when we go to see her, she is planning some party or getting ready to go to the Grand Tetons for a week of snow camping.

With all the stress and tension going on in our house, it's no wonder I prefer to be at school. Same goes for all of my friends. We all think our families are too busy or too frazzled or too crazy or too worked up about everything else. That's why we're all so glad to get to school so we can hang out with normal people for a while.

Our teachers are great, too. Except for one – Mr. Hopkins. Or Humpty Dumpty Hopkins, which is what we call him. He runs the computer lab. I think they put him in there because he only knows how to relate to computers. He certainly doesn't know how to relate to kids. I'm always getting detentions from Mr. Hopkins!

For instance, the week before winter break, he was making us go through some stupid computer program, step by step as if we were all super dummies!

"Okay, put the cursor at the top of the page..."

Now, thinking about words is my special thing, and I think that most words that have anything to do with computers are ridiculous. So, I just looked as serious as I could and said in my sweetest voice, "Excuse me, Mr. Hopkins..."

"Yes, Charlotte?" he answered impatiently.

"Why is it called a cursor? Is it because you have to use bad language to make it do what you want it to do?" I asked innocently.

The other kids started to chuckle, but no one laughed out loud. Humpty Dumpty Hopkins has a terrible temper when he gets going.

On this occasion, he just rolled his eyes and said, "You're holding me up, Charlotte..."

I muttered quietly, "Nah, your legs are doing that, Mr. Hopkins." But I thought I'd only said it loud enough for kids sitting near me to hear. Unfortunately Mr. Hopkins had super-human ears as well as a super-human temper.

"Charlotte Weisner! I think it's time for you to visit the detention room again!" he bellowed at me.

That time Mr. Hopkins gave me so much extra work to do I thought I'd never get home in time for winter break!

Chapter 2

The Bombshell Is Dropped

Looking back, I guess this whole story really starts on January 14, which was supposed to be one of those extra special days.

You see, January 14 was my birthday. And I'd always thought that people were supposed to be extra nice to you on your birthday. I'd always thought birthdays were filled with presents and parties and everything. So I woke up that morning feeling pretty excited. I sat up in bed and said to myself, "This is going to be one super-cool day!"

Little did I know how wrong that was going to be! Wrong megamillion times!

I should have known something was in the wind by what happened at breakfast time. First of all, Dad wasn't in a hurry to get off to work. That was pretty odd by itself. Besides that, Dad and Mom were acting really strange. They said they had a wonderful family surprise for both Nat and me, but they wouldn't tell us what it was until dinner. Of course that only made me think I was in for something really REALLY special for my birthday.

When I told my friends, they all agreed. "It must be something big!"

"Could it be a car?" asked Opu.

"You must be joking!" I said. "I'm only twelve! I'm not going to be allowed to drive for another four years!"

"What about a bigger bedroom?" asked Claudie. "You could use a little more space."

"Maybe you're all going to fly down to Disneyland for the weekend!" said Brett.

That sounded like a possibility. But then I thought that Dad would never do that. People only go to Disneyland to enjoy themselves, and Dad's forgotten how.

Claudie said, "Maybe they're going to buy you a horse."

I liked the sound of that idea.

"That's impossible," said Brett. "If you're going to get a horse, you have to have a barn and a field where it could run around."

"We do have a front lawn!" I said, and everyone started to laugh.

"Your front lawn is way too small for an animal as big as a horse!" Jamie howled.

Then Brett had to pipe up with some piece of useless information: "Do you know that a horse can run at speeds of up to forty miles an hour?"

"No we didn't know that," said Naiomi. "And we didn't really want to know it either!"

"Maybe Claudie's on the right track," Opu said. "Maybe you are getting an animal... What about a puppy?"

"That's it!" I said. "It has to be a puppy! Mom was in the basement the other day, rummaging through our old suitcases and things. I know we have an old basket down there. That's what she was looking for – a basket for the new puppy!"

We were all so excited at the idea of a new puppy that we started to think up a name for it.

"You don't want any of the usual names people give their dogs, like Rover or Champ or Spot," said Naiomi.

"What's wrong with Spot?" asked Claudie. "I kind of like Spot."

"But what if it doesn't have any spots?"

"Then you could call it Spotless!" said Jamie.

"Very funny!" I groaned.

"What about Scratch? That's something dogs sometimes do," Opu said with a laugh.

"I know what I want to call my birthday puppy!" I said. "I want to call her Duzz."

"Duzz? Why Duzz?" they asked.

"Because today I'm a dozen years old!"

Suddenly everyone was grinning. Duzz she was going to be. So that was that. All I had to do was act surprised when Mom and Dad broke the news about the puppy. After all, I didn't want to spoil their fun, did I?

That night, Dad and Mom took Nat and Grandma and me out for a family birthday party at my favorite restaurant. It's called *La casa de cena* and it has Mexican food. I love Mexican food, and what I love best of all are their chicken enchiladas and strawberry smoothies. They are just to die for!

So there I was, having a wonderful time. I was slurping on my strawberry smoothie and waiting for the big news about the puppy. In my mind I could just see myself saying, "Sit, Duzz!" "Heel, Duzz!" "Roll over, Duzz!"

Before dinner I'd found some sweaters that I never wear anymore for Duzz to curl up on when she goes to sleep on my bed at night. I'd even been practicing my whistling. I was all prepared.

When it was time for dessert, I had a fried ice cream, and Dad had sopapillas. He was in such a good mood, he was even cracking jokes!

"What is green and goes up and down, up and down?" he asked.

We all gave up on that one – even Nat.

"Simple," said Dad. "A head of lettuce in an elevator!"

We all groaned.

"Someone e-mailed me that today!" he said. Yes, Dad even has computerized jokes now – no wonder it wasn't funny.

Dad and Mom were getting more and more wound up. They were bursting to tell me the good news. I decided to encourage them a little.

"So what's going on, Dad?" I asked, and sat back to wait for the puppy announcement.

"Do you think we should tell them now?" Dad looked at Mom and winked.

"Oh, no," Mom answered teasingly. "I think we should leave it till the morning."

"For goodness sake!" I bellowed happily. "I need to know what my present is now, before I make a scene and embarrass you all."

"You do that on a daily basis anyway," Nat the Nerd said.

"All right," Dad said. "Your mother and I have a really special treat for everyone."

The "everyone" threw me at first, but then I thought that it would make sense if everyone else would enjoy having the puppy, even if that "everyone" else included Nat. With any luck, the puppy wouldn't like him anyway!

"Except poor old Grandma..." Dad continued merrily.

While Grandma reached over to thump Dad, I thought that this also made sense, since a puppy might get under her feet, which could cause her to fall and reinjure her knees.

"It's a very big present!" Mom said.

"Tell us, for goodness sake!" I shrieked.

Mom smiled and said, "Your father is being sent to New Zealand to set up a new software program for a firm. He has to stay six months so he can show the people how to use it."

I was thinking, "Okay, so while he's away we'll get this puppy…"

"So your mother and I thought it would be a great idea," Dad continued, "if we all went to New Zealand together!"

I dropped my spoon.

Nat gasped.

Were they out of their minds?

"You want us to go to – where?" I gasped.

Dad was beaming. "New Zealand. It's a beautiful country down near Australia."

"I don't care if it's right next door to the world's largest amusement park! What about school?" I asked.

"You'll go to school there," Dad said.

"But what about my friends?"

"Your father will get you a computer, and you can send them e-mail whenever you want to!" Mom said happily.

"A computer?" I thundered. "Haven't you noticed something? Charlotte Elizabeth Weisner does not do computers! I hate computers!"

"It's only for six months," Dad said.

"Six months is practically a lifetime. No one will recognize me when I come back. I'll be like Rip van Winkle! I'll walk around Boston and everyone will stare at me and wonder who I am!"

"You're being ridiculous now, Charlotte," said Mom, in her warning voice.

"This whole idea's ridiculous!" I said, and I slapped my hand down on the table so hard it made everyone's plate clink. I think it may have startled other people in the restaurant, too, but I didn't care.

But Dad did. He was obviously embarrassed. "I hope you realize you're making a fool of yourself, young lady!"

"I hope you realize you've ruined my birthday!" I said. "You've probably ruined my whole life!"

I could feel my voice choking in the back of my throat. I pushed my chair back so it grated on the floor, and I stood up. I was just about to run out to the car when suddenly the waiters rushed up to our table carrying a birthday cake with twelve bright

candles blazing on top. They began to sing in cheerful voices, "Happy birthday to you! Happy birthday to you! Happy birthday, dear Charlotte…"

I could feel the tears running down my cheeks. Even Nat was upset! Some birthday! I have the most clueless parents in the world!

Chapter 3

Doom! Doom! Doom!

The next morning I didn't want to get out of bed. I didn't even want to open my eyes.

"I'm sick!" I told Mom.

"You don't look sick to me, Charlotte. You just look like you're still feeling sorry for yourself."

"I've got plenty to feel sorry for myself about!"

"You have five minutes to get downstairs, or I'm pitching your yogurt," Mom threatened.

"What kind of yogurt is it?" I asked.

"Strawberry."

"You can't throw away strawberry yogurt! It's my favorite!"

"Five minutes," Mom said and walked away.

I crawled out of bed and dragged myself to the mirror. By the time I got to breakfast, Dad had already left for the airport. He was off to Minnesota for a few days. Mom was rushing to get to work because the spring jeans and shirts were coming in to the shop on the morning delivery truck. Nat was sitting in front of a bowl of cornflakes. But he wasn't really eating them. Instead, he was tracing lines in the cornflakes with his spoon.

"Mom," he said eventually.

"What, Nat?" Mom asked in a rushed voice.

"I've been thinking…"

"Now there's a first!" I muttered.

For once, Nat ignored me. "When you go to New Zealand…," he began.

"When *we* go to New Zealand," Mom corrected him.

"The point is, Grandma's going to be lonely when we're over there…"

Mom stopped bustling and turned to listen.

"…What I thought is, rather than going with you, why don't I stay and keep Grandma company?" he finished in a rush.

Nat was on to something here. "That's right!" I added eagerly. "She'll be heartbroken. Nat and I could stay and keep her company. She'd really like that. Maybe we could get her a puppy, too. Just to keep her company when we're at school."

I could see Nat glaring at me.

"I'm afraid that's out of the question," Mom said. "Grandma has a fabulous Florida vacation planned for this spring."

"I don't mind Florida…" I began.

"School!" Mom said. "Now!"

I told my friends the bad news on the way to school in the bus. They were as horrified as I was. Claudie said it was a plot to separate us.

Opu vowed she would write every other day!

Naiomi got very quiet, and I could see she was going to cry.

Brett said, "New Zealand is nine thousand miles away, or fifteen thousand kilometers as the crow flies, but of course crows don't fly because there's all that ocean and crows aren't seabirds, and besides crows would never fly that far!"

I figured this was Brett's way of saying he was on my side.

"So in other words, it's way too far away, right?" I asked him.

"Too far to swim anyway," he responded.

"Let's start a petition," Claudie suggested.

"Or a revolution!" Jamie added.

"Against who?" I asked.

"Against our parents!" Jamie said.

"But it's only Charlotte's parents who are taking her away," Brett reminded him. "There's no point in the rest of us revolting against our parents, is there?"

"I know," said Opu. "Charlotte could go on a hunger strike, and refuse to eat another thing till her parents agree to let her stay in Boston!"

I don't know why but I couldn't help thinking about a plate of chicken enchiladas and strawberry smoothies.

I shook my head. "No," I said. "I don't think I'm really hunger strike material. I'm just going to have to sulk so much that they'll want to change their minds."

It didn't work.

I thought I'd go see if Nat had come up with any great ideas on how NOT to go to New Zealand. For once I thought Nat and I could agree about something. Maybe if we both ganged up on Mom and Dad they might change their minds. When I pushed his door open, he was doing something on his computer.

"About this New Zealand thing...," I began.

Nat didn't look up. He just kept clicking away with his stupid mouse.

"What do you think we should do?"

"They have sixty million sheep!" he said.

"What?" I asked.

"In New Zealand. Sixty million sheep. That's a lot of sheep for a little country. They also have some strange birds and a lizard that is actually a living dinosaur. It sounds like a cool place."

I couldn't believe what I was hearing. "Well it didn't take you long to sell out, did it?" I asked and stormed out, slamming his door.

The two weeks before our big departure flew by. I'd given up pouting, mainly because Mom and Dad were just ignoring me – surprise, surprise. I could have been at death's door, and they wouldn't have noticed.

The day before we left – "Doomsday" as I had started to call it – my friends and I went to the mall for the last time. I said I'd send them my address as soon as we got there, and we all vowed to write letters every day. Then we did our special group handshake. Opu drew a Canadian goose on my arm, and I said I wasn't going to wash it off until I got back. Claudie said we needed some kind of memento to show we were best friends.

"I know!" said Brett. "We should get a group photograph."

There's a Take-Your-Own-Photo booth in our mall. We all squeezed in and made faces while the machine snapped away. I was glad we were laughing so hard, because I knew if we weren't I'd be crying.

The cab ride to Logan Airport was the most miserable in my whole life. Snow was falling again. I couldn't help hoping the airport would be closed, and we wouldn't be able to fly out.

But it wasn't. There were lots of people arriving for our flight. We stood in line with our bags. If only we were flying to Disneyland or somewhere we could have fun! Then I could have enjoyed all the excitement. Instead, I was going to have to sit on a plane for hours and hours. Days in fact, because even though we'd get on the plane Saturday afternoon Boston time, we wouldn't get to New Zealand until Monday morning New Zealand time! Somehow we'd lose a day somewhere.

"Charlotte can have the seat by the window for the first leg to Los Angeles," Mom said, as we boarded the plane.

"I don't care," I said. "I'm not going to look out anyway. I don't care about anything until we're in Boston again."

"Suit yourself," Dad said.

Nat sat next to me. Mom and Dad were in the two seats behind us. As we took off, I noticed Nat holding the arms of his seat tightly.

"Chicken!" I hissed.

"I am not!" he said.

Despite what I'd said to Dad, I did look out as we turned around and flew back over Boston. The glass was cold against my forehead. Below, the city looked as if it was covered in a layer of white icing, and it almost glowed under the late afternoon light. The John Hancock Tower was easy to make out. So was the Charles River, snaking its way through the town. And there, just for a few seconds, I was sure I could see our house. I peeked back through the seats to tell Mom.

But I didn't. Dad was already setting up his laptop to do some business stuff. Mom, however, had her face to the window. She looked as if she was searching for our house, too. There were tears in her eyes.

Chapter 4

G'day! Welcome to New Zealand!

"Good morning. Would you like the fruit plate or the omelet for breakfast?"

I woke up to find the flight attendant standing over me. The cabin glowed with a strange pink light. I glanced out the window. It was dawn and the sky was bright red.

"Fruit plate, please," I answered.

I ate my breakfast eagerly. I wasn't happy about where I was going, but that didn't mean I had to arrive feeling hungry!

Nat had the window seat, and he was looking out to see if he could catch sight of land. He also had a map on his lap.

"Are you worried the pilot might overshoot the country?" I asked.

Nat ignored me.

"Well I'm not going to look! I don't want to see any part of New Zealand," I said and put my nose in the air. But as we were coming down to land, I couldn't help taking a little peek. We were flying over some islands. Soon we began to see the city. Everything looked so green and fresh.

Before we started our descent, Dad had combed his hair and put on a tie. We were going to be met by his new boss, and he wanted to make a good impression.

We collected our bags, made our way through customs, and passed out of the airport into bright sunshine.

"Are you all right?" Mom asked me.

"It's so hot!" I complained.

"It's summer here, silly. Why don't you take off your coat?"

"I may as well leave it on," I said. "I'm catching the first plane back to Boston."

We went out into the main terminal. Straight ahead we saw a man holding up a sign saying "Weisner Family." He was wearing shorts and a bright red shirt. He hadn't bothered to shave, and he was actually wearing plastic sandals. Was this Dad's new boss? Mr. Casual Guy had even brought his kids with him.

"G'day," he said, shaking everyone's hand, including mine. "I'm Kevin and these are my kids, Sophie and Adam."

His children nodded shyly.

I figured handshaking was something people did in this country so I held out my hand to Sophie. She didn't seem to know what to do at first, but then took my hand limply. Adam just blushed when I took his hand and snatched it away before I could give it a good shake.

"Did they give you breakfast on the flight?" Dad's new boss asked.

"Oh yes, Kevin," I said.

"Mr. Lyons," Mom hissed in my ear as she poked me in the ribs.

I tried to ignore this and went on, "We had a choice of a fruit plate or omelet."

Kevin, a.k.a. Mr. Lyons, laughed. Not that I could see what he was laughing at – unless it was at his wild outfit. And as for the way he talked...

"It's gonna be a beaut day!" he enthused.

"It is?" Dad asked.

I was obviously going to have to learn a foreign language! It was bad enough, what with everything being so different. For a start, it was winter back home, but here it was summer with the sun glaring

down. Back home it was Sunday, but here it was Monday morning. People's accents were wildly different, and even worse, they called things by different names. When we got to his car, Mr. Lyons said, "Right, let's toss your bags in the boot."

I scrunched up my nose and said, "Huh? In your boot? What size do you wear?"

Mr. Lyons opened up the trunk and pointed. "We call this a boot down here."

Then, when we got to the car, Dad accidentally tried to get in the driver's side. That's because the steering wheel was on the wrong side! I was beginning to think everything was back to front or the wrong way around!

The company had rented a house for us in a suburb called Epsom. It was a fairly small house with a huge front porch. It was made of wood and the roof was covered with sheets of metal. All around the house was lawn and a few huge trees.

"I thought I'd let you have a bit of a look round and settle in. The house's all furnished and there are towels in the cupboard so you can have a shower or whatever. I only live down the road so I'll come back in about an hour and a half and take you out for some lunch."

Dad and Mom thanked him. He and the two kids got back in the car.

"Well?" asked Dad.

Mom grinned and squeezed his hand. "It's perfect!" she said.

I folded my arms across my chest and frowned hard. "It's too hot!"

"It's summer! It's supposed to be hot."

"The house has a metal roof!" I said.

"What's wrong with that?" asked Dad. "Lots of houses have metal roofs in this country."

"If it rains at night, we'll never get to sleep because it will be so noisy pounding away above our heads. And all this grass! I bet there are snakes everywhere!"

"There are no snakes at all in New Zealand," Nat said, as he started carrying luggage up the porch stairs.

"Sure, Nat – I bet there are!" I snapped.

"Nope," he said. "I looked it up on my CD-ROM encyclopedia."

"Then your CD-ROM is CD wrong!"

Mom, sick of the way this conversation was progressing, hauled me upstairs. "This is going to be your room, Charlotte. See? You even have a view of One Tree Hill," she said.

"It's an old volcano," know-it-all Nat said from behind her. "All the hills around this city are old volcanoes."

"Great!" I said. "With our luck they'll erupt while we're here and bury us in molten lava."

"Let's let Charlotte look around her room," Mom said, as she steered Nat and Dad out.

After they were gone, I slumped onto the bed. Dad had carried my suitcase in and set it on the floor at my feet. I looked around my room. The bed was huge. The curtains were light and gauzy. The floor was just shiny floorboards. By my bed was a sheepskin rug. I took off my shoes and felt it with my feet. It felt warm and spongy.

Over by the window was a small desk. I started to unpack some of my special things: a rock Brett had brought back for me from his family vacation in Greece, a stuffed grizzly bear Grandma had given me when I was a baby, and one of the photos we had taken of ourselves in the Take-Your-Own Photo booth at the mall.

Mom came back into my room. I ignored her and dumped some more stuff on the desk.

"You'll need some space on your desk to do your homework," she said.

"I'm not going to have any homework!" I said, pouting.

"Oh, I'm sure you will," Mom said.

"Oh, I'm sure I won't!" I said. "Because I'm not going to go to school!"

Chapter 5

School Is Not Cool!

"Class, I'd like you all to help Charlotte settle in and find her way round. Charlotte comes from America. I'm sure she'll have lots of interesting things to tell us about her country."

I could feel all these eyes looking at me. There were thirty-five kids in the class, too, so that's a lot of eyes. And they were all wearing the same clothes. They call it a school uniform. "Uniform" is right! It makes them all look the same. The boys were wearing blue shirts and gray pants. The girls wore blue shirts and a gray skirts. In the winter, when it is cold out, they put on a bright blue sweater. Only they don't call it a sweater. They call it a jumper.

Mom had to buy a school uniform for me, too, even though I was only going to be at the school for six months. She said she didn't want me to feel different from the other kids.

"But I am different!" I said. "Sometimes I think I even speak a different language!"

The classrooms looked different, too. They didn't sit in rows like schools back in Boston always made us do. Instead they pushed their desks together and made big tables with them.

"I've got an empty desk next to me," said one of the girls. "Come and sit by me."

"Thank you, Ngaire," said the teacher.

"That's me," whispered the girl. "I'm Ngaire."

"Hi there," I whispered back.

It was the start of a new term. In fact it was the start of a new year because New Zealand schools start up in February, which is the end of their summer vacation. Everyone wanted to talk about all the exciting things they had been doing – especially the swimming. Ngaire had stayed on a farm with one of her uncles (where she got to swim in a lake). A few kids had gone to Australia (and they swam in the ocean). But most had stayed home and gone swimming at one of the zillions of beaches around the city. I was beginning to think that instead of getting summer vacations like American kids, they got "swimming vacations"!

"What about you, Charlotte? Would you like to tell the class about what you did on your holidays?" It was the teacher again. Her name is Mrs. Caulfield. She seemed nice, but she didn't appear

38

to be in any hurry to get on to some real work. There wasn't a worksheet in sight.

"Well," I said, "I don't know because back home, we've been in school for over a month now. And since I'm already settled there, just being here is pretty weird. In fact, I'm not even sure I'm staying. I'm hoping to catch the first plane back."

"Oh?" asked Mrs. Caulfield, looking surprised. "I understood from your mother that you were going to be with us for at least six months."

"That's my mother for you," I said. "She exaggerates."

The other children laughed. Mrs. Caulfield just nodded. Then she turned to another kid.

The morning seemed to fly by. Then a bell rang. The teacher told us to pack up our things and go outside. I waited for her to follow us so she could supervise us during the break. But instead of coming with us, she went off with the teacher from the next classroom.

"They're going to the staffroom, silly," said Ngaire. "It's play time."

"Huh?" I asked, following Ngaire into the little room where all our bags and coats were kept. "And what are we supposed to do?"

"We play, of course. And eat our play lunch."

"What's a play lunch? Is that a pretend lunch?" I asked, worried.

"Don't tell me your mother didn't give you any?" Ngaire was getting concerned now. "It's something to eat. Like morning tea," she said.

"You mean a snack?" I asked.

"I suppose so," Ngaire said.

"No. She didn't give me anything," I said. "Was she supposed to?"

"Well yes, unless you don't get hungry in the morning," Ngaire said, reaching into her school bag. "But she did give you your lunch, didn't she?" she added.

"Lunch?" Now I was starting to worry, too. I can't survive all day without my lunch! "No," I said. "But I can just get lunch in the school cafeteria, can't I? With all the other kids?"

Ngaire started to laugh. "We don't have a school cafeteria!" she said. "We bring our lunches from home."

I was beginning to get upset now.

"Don't worry," said Ngaire cheerfully. "I'll share mine with you." She pulled out a small package wrapped in plastic wrap. "Dad makes my lunch, and he always gives me too much to eat. I'll give you half my biscuit for now."

"Biscuit?" I asked.

Ngaire unwrapped the plastic wrap to reveal a large cookie with nuts sticking out of it. She snapped it in half and gave me a piece to try.

"Delicious," I said. "Did your mom buy this?"

"Oh, no," said Ngaire. "She made it." Ngaire took a big bite out of her cookie.

"Made it?" I said. "Do you mean she baked it herself?"

"My mum loves baking," said Ngaire. "Come on! I'll show you how to play patter tennis."

After lunch I was in for a real shock. When we got back into the classroom, Mrs. Caulfield was holding a silver whistle.

"Time for swimming," she said.

"Did you bring your togs?" Ngaire asked.

"My what?"

"For swimming? Your swimming togs."

"You mean my swimsuit?" I asked nervously. "No, I didn't bring it. Was I supposed to?"

"Our class has swimming lessons every second day during the warmer months."

"And you have to wear your swimsuits in front of the boys?" I gasped.

"Well, you can go swimming in the buff if you like," Ngaire giggled.

I turned to find Mrs. Caulfield standing beside me.

"I'm sorry, Charlotte," she said. "I forgot to remind your mother about the swimming."

"Oh, that doesn't matter," I said. "I won't need to go swimming anyway. I can already swim pretty well." I smiled sweetly at Mrs. Caulfield and hoped it would make the whole swimming nightmare go away.

She looked at me in a funny way and said, "Really? Then you'll be able to help the other children who aren't very good at it yet."

This wasn't what I had in mind!

"I'd love to, Mrs. Caulfield," I said, "but my mother doesn't like me to swim in public swimming pools."

"That's funny, dear," she said. "You see, she told me she was delighted to hear you would be learning to swim. She said you weren't very confident in the water yet."

Isn't that just like a mother? They tell complete strangers the most embarrassing things about you!

"Bring your swimming togs tomorrow, dear, okay?" Mrs. Caulfield said, and walked away.

"If it's any consolation," said Ngaire, "I'm a hopeless swimmer, too!"

"It's not that I'm hopeless…," I said, trying to cover my embarrassment. "I think Americans swim differently. You know – kind of like how you guys drive on the other side of the road."

"So you swim on the other side of the pool?" Ngaire asked with a grin. "Come on! You'll be okay, I promise!" she said, and looped her arm through mine.

Two weeks later, I was starting to feel a little desperate. I still hadn't heard a thing from my friends back in Boston! What were they up to? I thought they were going to write every day! That's what they promised. So much for their extra serious oath! Of course I hadn't written to them, but that's because I'd been waiting for them to write to me. And anyway, it seemed as if they should be the first ones to write because I was the one who'd been kidnapped by my family and taken thousands of miles across the Pacific!

Finally, in my desperation for any kind of American company, I decided to seek out my brother. Dinner was over, so I moseyed down the hall to his room.

His door was half-open, and I could see him standing in front of his mirror, holding his cricket bat in his hand. He was practicing hitting an imaginary cricket ball. He swung the bat wildly through the air and then gave a sort of whispered shout. "Four!"

"For what?" I asked.

Nat swung around. "Hey! Who said you could come snooping in my room?"

"I wasn't snooping. I was just mildly amused to see you parading in front of the mirror!"

"I wasn't parading!" he said in an irritated voice, although I could see he was actually just embarrassed. "I was practicing my cricket strokes, thank you very much."

"Hmm!" I said.

I looked around his room. I hadn't been in his room for a couple of days.

"Where'd you get all the posters?" I asked. He had music posters all over his walls and even some taped on the ceiling.

"One of the boys in my math class gave them to me. His father owns a CD store, and they get them all the time. Awesome, aren't they? There's the Rhubarb Rockers, the Purple Termites, and my favorite, Bingo and the Baked Bean Band."

"Those are the bands' names?" I asked. "They sound about as weird as you!"

"They've all got pages on the web, too. Want to see them? Bobby Bingo's got a lot of neat stuff, including some sound files!" Nat pointed to his computer.

That only made me mad.

"How many times do I have to tell people in this family? I do not do computers! I hate computers! If Dad wasn't a computer geek, I wouldn't be down here in this country, having to go to school with kids who use words I've never heard of and do everything different!"

I stamped out and slammed his door.

Chapter 6

The Box

The day after this, I finally had to go swimming. I'd been pretty lucky for two weeks because the weather had been cold and rainy, but the sun had come back and there was no way I could get out of it (and I certainly tried!).

First, I tried leaving my swimming things at home. I picked up my bag and left my swimming suit and towel behind on the table.

I got as far as the gate. Mom came running after me. "You forgot something," she panted.

I wondered about letting it fall out of my bag as I walked to school. But Ngaire came running up to join me.

"Great! You have your togs!" she said. "It's going to be a hot day. You'll love it in the water."

Love it, I did not! Swimming was one big humiliation from start to finish! First there was the waiting for it to happen part. All morning I just sat there and dreaded it. But it wasn't until we came back to class after lunch that I saw Mrs. Caulfield standing there, holding her silver whistle. I knew what that meant!

"Okay, class, go ahead to the changing rooms. You have five minutes," she said.

I have to tell you that the girl's changing room isn't much bigger than my closet back home, so when there are fifteen bodies in there, all trying to get their clothes off without anyone seeing their undies or anything, you get some idea about how terrible it was. The only thing that sort of made it bearable was the noise and the giggling. It turned out that my swimsuit was different than everyone else's, so of course they had to keep asking me questions about it.

I was feeling so uncomfortable I just wanted to get out of there. As soon as I was ready, I walked out into the hallway and went over to one of the doors that I thought led to the pool. I said to Ngaire, "Come on! Let's get it over with!"

"Wait!" Ngaire said.

But I ignored her. If she wasn't ready, too bad. I wrapped my towel around my body tightly and yanked the door open. I instantly realized why Ngaire had said to wait. The door swung back and immediately I was greeted by a loud chorus of yells and lots of pink and brown boyish bodies all

scurrying to cover themselves! How was I to know the boys were getting changed in there?

Ngaire dragged me away, giggling her head off. The other girls thought it was cool, too.

"Did you actually see them naked?" Jennifer Cooper asked.

"Who cares?" I asked. But I was still burning up with embarrassment. "Why don't they have better signs on the doors?" I asked.

"Well, we've never had a problem figuring out where to go," Winnie said, still giggling helplessly.

The pool was very small, only about as wide as my bedroom back in Boston and about three times as long.

Mrs. Caulfield lined us up alongside the pool and then counted us off into groups. I noticed she hadn't changed into her swimsuit – she was going to teach us how to swim from outside the pool. Everyone else put their towels down on the grass beside the pool, but I kept mine tightly wrapped around me, making sure as little as possible of me was visible.

"You won't need your towel till after we get out," Mrs. Caulfield said.

"I'm actually feeling a little cold, Mrs. Caulfield," I said. "I must have a chill coming on. I think I'll watch the swimming today. I can learn just as much that way."

Mrs. Caulfield simply smiled and said, "It's a lovely, warm day today, Charlotte." She calmly but firmly took my towel from me, folded it up, and dropped it on the grass beside the others.

"Now, everyone in the pool."

With squeals and shouts they all jumped or slid into the water. I couldn't move.

"Come on," Ngaire said, "the water's really warm today!"

The lesson part wasn't too bad. My group had to do things like hold on to the handrail and put our heads under the water and blow bubbles. Then we had to float. It turned out I'm pretty good at floating. Mrs. Caulfield started to clap and the other kids did, too – even though they can all swim really well.

Mrs. Caulfield always expected us to do lots of work ourselves. Within a few weeks after my arrival, we were already working on our group projects. There were four people in our group. There were Ngaire and me, and two boys: Rua, who sings like Elvis Presley; and Sefi, who is from Tonga.

First, Mrs. Caulfield took the whole class to the Kelly Tarlton Underwater Aquarium. That was awesome. There was a section all about Antarctica, and then we stood on a moving walkway and went through an underwater tunnel. Fish swam over our heads and to the sides of us.

Then, each group had to choose a subject for "investigation." It was kind of like being a detective. We had to find out as much as we could and then come up with some hunches of our own. Then we had to present all this in some kind of book or publication.

Our group chose to study the yellow-eyed penguin because it looks really cute, and it's also an endangered species.

One day early on in the project, Ngaire and I went to the library together after school. Some other kids from our class were there, too. Rua had turned up but Sefi wasn't able to. He has two younger brothers and a younger sister, and he has to help at home after school.

We found some good books on yellow-eyed penguins and photocopied some pictures we could use for our project. When we had what we needed, Rua suggested we photocopy our hands.

"How?" I asked.

"We all just put our hands on the glass and hit the copy button."

Ngaire began to giggle. "Yes, lets! Sometimes it looks really weird!"

So Rua and Ngaire and I all put our right hands on the glass plate. Rua put the money in with his other hand and started the machine.

"Cool! It looks like seaweed!" Ngaire said.

We did two more, so we each had one. I noticed in the last copy that one of Ngaire's fingers was touching one of Rua's.

I'd told Mom I'd be home by 5:30, so when the library clock said a quarter of five, I gathered up my stuff.

Ngaire walked part of the way home with me. Suddenly she stopped in front of me and asked, "What do you think of Rua?"

"What do you mean?" I asked.

"I think he likes you," she said, and she gave me a poke in the ribs that sort of tickled.

"I don't LIKE him like him, if that's what you mean," I said slowly.

"Me neither," Ngaire said, but I wasn't sure I believed her.

"See you in the morning!" she said when she got to her gate. Then, without really looking at me, she said, "So, your friends in America... I guess you really miss them, don't you?"

"Like you wouldn't believe!" I said. "You can't imagine how great they all are – we hang around together so much that everyone calls us Charlotte's gang."

Ngaire shrugged her shoulders. "Then I guess they're your real friends, aren't they?"

"Well, sure they're my real friends – I've known them practically my whole life," I said, not understanding what she was trying to get at.

"Yeah," Ngaire said, then she ran up the drive.

I watched her go. I thought she'd turn and wave but she didn't. What had that been about? I asked myself. Then I clapped my hand to my forehead – what a dunce I can be! Poor Ngaire, all she had wanted was a little assurance that I like her, too. And it had been such a good day. Little did I know it was about to get worse!

When I got inside, Mom was waiting for me. "Your father has a surprise for you," she said with a weak grin. It was as if she was nervous or something. "He's in your bedroom. He's just getting it set up."

Uh-oh, I thought. I pushed open my door.

"Hi!" Dad said. He was sitting at my desk. All of the special things I had on my desk had been pushed to one side, and in their place there was a box with a screen on top and a keyboard in front!

"Dad!" I groaned. "What is that?"

"It's a computer," he said.

"I can see that!" I said warily. "But what is it doing on my desk?"

"It's yours," he said.

"Why?" I asked. "I didn't ask for it."

Dad just smiled and said, "They were replacing some of the old machines at work. This was going to be dumped so I thought you could use it."

"For what?"

"Whatever you like," he said. "I've set it up for you. You might like to do some of your schoolwork on it."

"Dad, with all of the hours you work, you may not have noticed," I said in the flattest voice I could muster, "but I do my schoolwork on paper, and a pen is all I need."

Dad just ignored this. "I've organized your own e-mail address, too," he said cheerfully.

"E-mail? I don't care if it's got A, B, or C mail! It's cluttering up my desk!"

"Your mom and I thought that since Nat has his own computer, you should have one, too."

"Nat and I have nothing in common," I said. "Nat is a hopeless nerd, and there is nothing that he has that I would want!"

Dad just laughed. "Suit yourself," he said. "This is where you turn it on." He pointed to a button on the front of the box.

I didn't even bother to look.

"I got you this old office chair, too. It swivels and you can adjust the height so you don't have to strain while you're working on the keyboard."

"Dad, I don't think there's going to be any strain because I'm not going to be using this computer," I said.

"Try the chair anyway," he encouraged.

I sat on the chair and swiveled back and forth. I knew Dad was waiting for me to thank him. But I just couldn't.

Chapter 7

Charlotte – Are You There!

The rest of that week, my life went from bad to worse. Ngaire asked our group up to her house to work on our penguin project. But when Rua turned up, she spent the whole time giggling at him, and paying no attention to me at all. As for our work on the yellow-eyed penguin – well, we didn't get anything done. When Sefi said he had to go, I went with him. We left Rua and Ngaire there, throwing wadded up pieces of paper at each other.

Sefi walked as far as my place with me. He's very quiet, but I can always talk enough for two people. Anyway, I was saying how unfair it was that I'd been dragged down here when Sefi stopped walking. He kicked a stone on the sidewalk (which they call a footpath here).

"It's hard when you come from another country," he said. "My family came from Tonga."

"Yes, I know," I said.

"Sometimes my mother sits out in the garden by herself and cries," he said.

"Why?"

"She's thinking about her home." Sefi was looking down at the ground.

"Is she always sad when she thinks of her home?" I asked.

"Oh, no!" said Sefi. "Not when all our relatives come to visit. Then she puts flowers in her hair and they sing and dance all night!"

When we got to my house, I said good-bye to Sefi and went inside. I immediately sensed that something was wrong. My bedroom door was shut, but I could hear voices inside.

Boy voices!

I pushed the door open and there, to my horror, was Nat with a group of his friends! They were sitting around, using my computer.

"What are you doing?" I snapped.

"I'm sorry," Nat said. "My computer crashed, and I can't get it back up. I'll have to get Dad to look at it. I thought you wouldn't mind if I checked out a few things with yours..."

The other guys were looking at me. I started to feel a little embarrassed about my outburst.

Then my nerd brother did something he's never done before – he actually introduced me to his friends.

"This is my sister, Charlotte," he said pleasantly. "And this is Dave and Steve and Yo." Nat started packing up his stuff.

"You can use it if you like," I said. "The computer... I really don't mind."

"We're finished, anyway," Nat said. "We were just messing around."

A sign came up on the screen saying, "It is now safe to turn off your computer." Nat pushed a button and the screen suddenly went blank.

"Let's play a game of cricket. There's enough room on our lawn," Nat said, leading the way.

As Yo was leaving my room, he said, "Do you know you have some e-mail waiting for you?"

"Oh, sure," I said, trying to sound cool. "I get so much e-mail, half the time I don't even bother to read it!" I laughed, expecting Yo to laugh, too.

But he just smiled and said, "Nat says you won't use your computer."

"Me?" I felt myself blushing. What had Nat been saying about me? "Maybe I use it when no one is looking," I said, trying to sound convincing.

Yo just looked at me.

"All right!" I said grouchily. "So I haven't used it for a while. But I could if I wanted to!"

"Do you want me to help you?" Yo asked. "I wouldn't mind, really. You start it up, and I'll help you when you get stuck."

I was obviously digging myself a deeper and deeper hole.

"Tell you what," I said. "Why don't you do it for me. That way I'll remember it all."

"Oh, no," said Yo. "You never remember when other people do it for you. You have to do it yourself. That way you don't just remember with your brain. Your hands remember, too."

I looked at Yo. I wasn't going to get out of this!

"Okay," I said.

I sat down on my swivel chair and swung to and fro. Yo knelt on the floor beside me.

"I know what to do first!" I said breezily. "I turn it on! Anyone can do that!" I poked a button on the front of the box. Nothing happened.

"That's the reset button," Yo said, trying not to smile. "The power button's the one below."

"I knew that! I was just joking around!"

I poked the power button and things began to happen. The computer made a whirring noise and things appeared on the screen.

"Now what?" I asked.

"Wait until it's finished booting up," Yo said.

"Booting up?" I asked. "Now isn't that funny. In my country we don't call it booting up. In fact we don't even have boots on our cars. We call them trunks. So in the United States we call this trunking up."

Yo just looked at me and smiled. "You're kidding around again, huh?" he asked.

Soon the screen stopped changing. Off to one side of it, there were these things that looked like badges or shields.

I knew I had to do something with the mouse, but I didn't know what.

"Click the dial-up icon," Yo suggested.

"Of course," I said, frantically looking for something that said "icon" or "dial-up."

Yo pointed to a little picture on the screen. I moved the cursor there and clicked.

"You have to double click," said Yo.

I clicked two times. Once again things started to happen. Suddenly the screen showed a box with a whole list of names. I gasped. I could see names I knew – Claudie, Opu, Naiomi, Brett, Jamie... Jamie again. Jamie again. Claudie again... And then there was one from "The Gang."

"You have fourteen messages," Yo said. "You must be a very popular person."

"Oh, that's nothing!" I drawled. "Sometimes I get thirty or more!"

"Charlotte, why don't you just read them?" he asked wryly. "All you need to do is click on one and the message will appear."

"I was just going to do that," I said. I moved the cursor to one called "The Gang" and clicked.

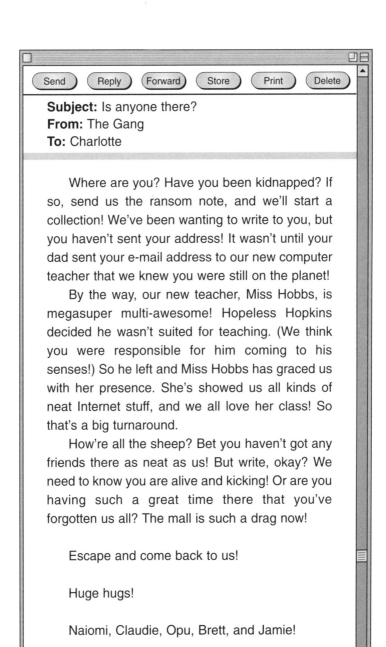

Send   Reply   Forward   Store   Print   Delete

Subject: Is anyone there?
From: The Gang
To: Charlotte

Where are you? Have you been kidnapped? If so, send us the ransom note, and we'll start a collection! We've been wanting to write to you, but you haven't sent your address! It wasn't until your dad sent your e-mail address to our new computer teacher that we knew you were still on the planet!

By the way, our new teacher, Miss Hobbs, is megasuper multi-awesome! Hopeless Hopkins decided he wasn't suited for teaching. (We think you were responsible for him coming to his senses!) So he left and Miss Hobbs has graced us with her presence. She's showed us all kinds of neat Internet stuff, and we all love her class! So that's a big turnaround.

How're all the sheep? Bet you haven't got any friends there as neat as us! But write, okay? We need to know you are alive and kicking! Or are you having such a great time there that you've forgotten us all? The mall is such a drag now!

Escape and come back to us!

Huge hugs!

Naiomi, Claudie, Opu, Brett, and Jamie!

I couldn't help it. At first I wanted to laugh and tell Yo about my friends and the crazy stuff we used to do – but then I suddenly knew if I said anything at all, I was going to cry. Yo must have known this, too. He didn't look at me. Instead, looking down at the keyboard, he said, "If you like, I'll write down some instructions and then you can write a reply to all your friends."

I nodded. My cheeks were burning. All I could think of was Claudie and Naiomi and Opu and Brett and Jamie – they hadn't forgotten about me after all.

That night after dinner, I didn't watch any television. Instead, I told Mom I had to do some extra homework. Mom looked puzzled.

Nat said, "Oh, sure you do, you joker!"

I went straight to my room, closed the door, and sat down at my desk. I picked up Yo's instructions. They were so neatly written. I looked at the blank computer screen. I could see my reflection. I shrugged my shoulders, took a big breath, and reached for the button labeled power...

Chapter 8

Charlotte the Mighty Has Fallen!

How could this have happened? Despite all of my best intentions, before I knew it, I was regularly e-mailing my friends back in Boston.

Yes, I'd started using the stupid computer!

And what was worse – and I really hated to admit this – I'd actually become something of an e-mail addict! The first thing I did when I got up in the morning was turn on the computer to see who had written to me. And then I rushed home from school just so I could turn it on and check my e-mails again!

Naiomi was very impressed with my learning to swim. She said we'd hit the beaches when I get home – she had a huge case of spring fever going.

Jamie said he was collecting information for a report he had to write on sheep, and he asked me a million questions about the stupid animals. Do merino sheep have curled horns? Who is the current New Zealand champion sheep shearer? How long does it take to shear a sheep? Are there women sheep shearers? What is a "jumbuck"?

Claudie said Naiomi was setting the school sports world on fire. Naiomi said it was no big deal.

Opu said she'd sent some drawings in an e-mail and that it was on something she called an attached file – whatever that meant. I had to wait until Yo came over to visit Nat again so I could ask him to help me with that.

As for our yellow-eyed penguin book – we had entered the panic zone. We had to have it done by the following week, and we only had six days left! We didn't have our information together, and we didn't have enough drawings and illustrations. That was when I got bossy! I had everyone give me their notes so I could type them up on the computer. And after I'd said I never would... I guess it's like Grandma always says, "How the mighty have fallen!"

So, life was changing pretty fast. There was one Saturday in particular that stands out in my mind as being pretty bizarre – especially considering my family. Now, back home in Boston, Saturday was not much different than any other day. Usually Dad would work and Mom would rush off to the shop and I would be left with Nat and Grandma. But in New Zealand, people did things more slowly on Saturdays, and they got up in the morning intent on enjoying themselves. They'd go shopping, or play sports, or watch other people play sports.

So it was a surprise when on that one Saturday, Dad woke us up at the crack of dawn with an almighty bellow.

"Come on, guys! Up and at 'em! We leave in half an hour."

I poked my head into the hallway. There was Dad, already dressed – if you could call it that! He was wearing a bright orange shirt that was even more obnoxious than the one his boss had worn when he met us at the airport. He also had on loud, baggy shorts, and he looked ridiculous with his spindly legs sticking out the bottom.

I stared at him. What had come over my father? Back in Boston, he would never have worn something like this. In fact he always seemed to wear the same boring suit, white shirt, and drab tie. Day in and day out. But this...?

"Dad!" I said. "I hope you're not going to appear in public wearing that!"

"Why not?" he asked.

"It's like pajamas! And why do we have to get up so early? There's no school today."

"We're going to my company's picnic," he said. "And I want to look the part!" Then he twirled to show off his unbelievable outfit.

The company's annual picnic – so that was it. I remembered now. Dad had mentioned it the previous Monday. I shivered at the thought of it. We were all going to be herded into buses with a bunch of complete strangers and driven to some beach place called Wenderholme.

"Don't forget to take your swimsuit," he said. "They say the beach is wonderful for swimming."

"Since you're in the spirit of the whole New Zealand thing, Dad, here swimsuits are called togs," I said, trying to think of a way I could get out of the picnic.

"Whatever!" said Dad. "Just move it! We have to be in the company parking lot by ten o'clock."

"Do I really have to go?" I asked.

"Do you want the short answer or the long answer?" asked Dad.

"Both," I said.

"The short answer is 'yes, you do have to go,' and the long answer is 'yes, you do have to go, so get moving!'"

He went to Nat's room before I could say any more, thumped on the door, and yelled, "Nat?"

"I'm moving!" Nat shouted back happily. Nat was really enjoying the whole shouting thing.

"You are in charge of all of our hats, towels, and beach toys," Dad said, still shouting.

"Great! No problem!" Nat said. "I'll bring my cricket gear, too."

"And if I have to go, what am I in charge of?" I asked.

"I think we'll put you in charge of bad attitudes and crabby faces!" Dad said. He had definitely flipped! I've never seen Dad as relaxed or as bellowingly cheerful as this! "Actually," he said, "you can load the picnic food in the cooler."

"You're wrong again, Dad!" I said, starting to get in the spirit of the thing in spite of myself. "In this country, a cooler is called a chilly-bin!"

"Well, fill it – whatever it's called!" he said, pushing me toward the kitchen.

"Hey," I protested, "it's sexist to make Mom and me take care of the food."

"I'm not making you and Mom do the food, Miss Feminist! You are doing the food and Mom is getting ready."

"Wrong!" Mom said, as she made a grand entrance in her brand-new swimsuit. "I am ready! What do you think?" she asked.

"Very cool, Mom," I said. "But that's not normal breakfast attire."

"Oh, I don't know, I kind of like it," Dad said, winking at Mom.

"Has everyone in this place gone completely nuts?" I asked.

We got to Dad's office at five minutes to ten. There were two big buses and lots of cars and people there. Everyone seemed to know everyone else, except me! Great! A whole day with no one to talk to except Nat, Mom, and Dad!

"There's Anne Marie," said Nat, running off to talk to her. Anne Marie is in his math class, and he talks about her all the time. Great, so now Nat was going to spend the whole day hanging around his would-be girlfriend and I was going to have no one to talk to all day! Not that I ever talk to Nat, but you don't feel like such a loser when you are with other people, even nerd brothers!

I was just about to ask my parents to put me in a taxi and send me home again, when someone touched my arm from behind.

"Hi, Charlotte."

I turned around. It was Yo!

"What are you doing here?" I asked.

"My mom works for the company, too," he said. "She's a programmer."

"Really?" I asked. And then for once I couldn't think of anything else to say. It was a pretty stupid time to become tongue-tied!

"My mom's on the other bus, so I'll see you at the picnic," he said.

"Yeah, right!" I fumbled.

He waved and headed back to the other bus.

"Come on," Dad said. "Time to head out."

"Can't we go on the other bus?" I asked.

"Nope," Dad said. "All our stuff is on this one, and your mother's already on board. It looks as if you'll have to sit by me and keep me company."

It took about an hour to get to Wenderholme, and about another hour to get the whole picnic set up. With all the running around, I didn't see Yo again until after lunch. I had gone into the changing sheds to put on my suit. I wasn't planning on swimming – the waves made me a little nervous – but it was very hot, and I thought I would at least be comfortable. As I came out of the sheds, I practically bumped into him.

"I'm just going in for another swim, too," he said, grinning. He was carrying a boogie-board.

"Well, I don't know..." I started to say.

"I have to use this," he said. "You see, I can't swim very well."

"You can't?" I asked.

Yo shook his head and looked embarrassed. "My mom and I didn't come to New Zealand until

71

I was in intermediate school. By then, everyone else had already learned how to swim."

"I can't swim either," I said. "But I'm learning. Maybe we could help each other out…"

"Okay," Yo said with a grin.

Well, for all of our agreements, no one could possibly swim in the sea anyway. No sooner did you try to float than a wave would come crashing over you! Still, Yo and I had a lot of fun with his boogie-board. To ride it, I had to hold on tight and hug it to me. Then the waves would pick me up and shoot me toward the beach.

We got home about nine o'clock that night. It turned out that Dad's boss could play the accordion, so all the way back everyone joined in a rowdy sing-along. I didn't know half the words, but it didn't seem to matter.

"Did you have a good day?" Dad asked when we got settled. He had his arm around Mom.

I was going to say something whiny about my sandfly bites – although I didn't have too many because I'd loaded on the insect repellent, or about how tired I felt. But I didn't.

"It was great – thanks, Dad," I said.

As I headed off to my bedroom, I reflected that I was glad I'd gone swimming after all – with the practice I was getting at school, I was starting to feel okay in the water. I knew I'd looked pretty goofy floundering around out there, but who hadn't? And even if Yo thought I looked silly, he did come back to the city in our bus – although he rode with nerdy Nat. There was so much to think about. Like why did Dad give me that great big hug when I thanked him for the fun day? Normally he just ruffles my hair or gives me a peck on the cheek. I wish people would tell me what's going on!

When I got to my room, I quietly closed the door and turned on the computer. I wanted to see if I had any e-mails from my friends.

Even though I was too tired to type much, I wanted to read what they had to say and to tell them to stand by because I was planning on giving them the whole lowdown on the picnic in the morning.

First I read my new messages. There was one from Naiomi saying, "Thank Goodness It Was Friday." There was also one from Jamie, thanking me for the information about sheep. And one from Opu that just said, "Chirp! Chirp!" plus the message, "File Attached."

And then I saw my last message.

I practically stopped breathing.

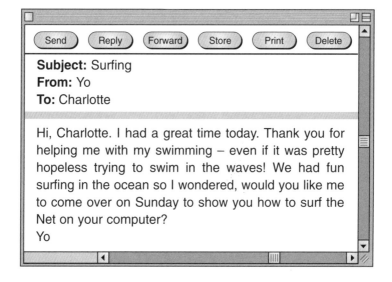

Subject: Surfing
From: Yo
To: Charlotte

Hi, Charlotte. I had a great time today. Thank you for helping me with my swimming – even if it was pretty hopeless trying to swim in the waves! We had fun surfing in the ocean so I wondered, would you like me to come over on Sunday to show you how to surf the Net on your computer?
Yo

I immediately clicked on the reply button and began to type.

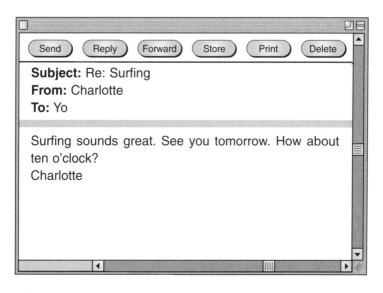

Subject: Re: Surfing
From: Charlotte
To: Yo

Surfing sounds great. See you tomorrow. How about ten o'clock?
Charlotte

74

Chapter 9

Surf's Up!

We all slept in on Sunday. I rolled over at about half past nine and saw the clock – whoops! I leaped out of bed, threw on some clothes, and ran down the hall to the kitchen. Mom looked out her bedroom door.

"What's going on? What's all the running about?" she said sleepily.

"Oh, I forgot. Someone's coming over."

"Ngaire doesn't normally get up this early on a Sunday morning."

"Mom, it's not Ngaire, okay?"

"So who is it?"

"Mom, I'm in a hurry... can I get the third degree later?"

"Well, dear," Mom said dryly, "it's just that if you are inviting some complete stranger to our house, it would be polite to let us know about it a little bit beforehand."

"He's not a complete stranger," I said, starting to get flustered. "He's been here before, and it's no big deal. All right?"

Now Nat the Nerd looked out of his doorway.

"Did I hear you say 'he'?"

Well, that did it.

"Mom! Look what you've done now – you woke up Drip van Winkle!"

"Go back to bed, Nat," Mom said, closing his door firmly, although I could hear Nat guffawing on the other side. "There are donuts in the jar on the counter, Charlotte."

"Thanks, but I'm not hungry, Mom."

"For your guest, silly!" she said, smiling understandingly.

Yo arrived at ten o'clock on the dot.

"I hope I'm not too early?" he asked.

"Nah," I said. "I've been up for ages."

I brought a chair from the kitchen to sit on while Yo used mine, but he insisted that I sit right in front of the computer so that I could really try out everything – not just watch him do the work.

"You probably know all about surfing the Net," Yo said.

"Well," I began, "back in Boston I used to do this sort of thing all the time."

Yo just looked at me.

"Okay, other people used to in my computer class at school. I didn't, though. You see, the teacher hated me – well, actually we hated each other. Anyway, I was usually banned from the computer lab." I was starting to feel a little embarrassed about all of my shenanigans in computer class, so I hurriedly said, "Would it be okay if you just start explaining what I need to know and see how far we get from there?"

For the next quarter of an hour we just talked computer stuff. Yo told me all about the World Wide Web, and browsers, and search engines. Before long, my head was spinning!

"Wait a minute! With all these new words, I'm going to have to start my own dictionary!" I said at one point.

Yo thought that was a good idea, too, so I started a file in my word-processing program, and I began to write up all these new words and what they basically meant. Yo said I should set it up as a table, so the computer could keep everything in alphabetical order for me. I asked how, and he showed me how to highlight the name column and then go to the table menu and tell it to sort it alphabetically.

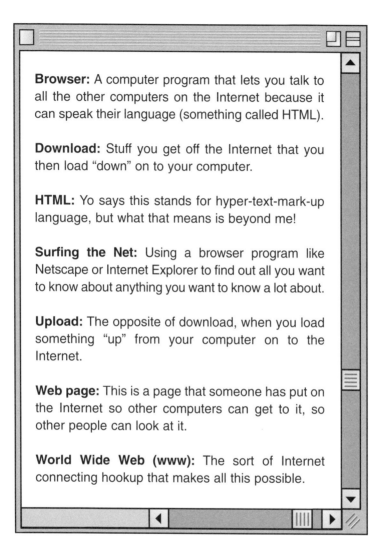

Browser: A computer program that lets you talk to all the other computers on the Internet because it can speak their language (something called HTML).

Download: Stuff you get off the Internet that you then load "down" on to your computer.

HTML: Yo says this stands for hyper-text-mark-up language, but what that means is beyond me!

Surfing the Net: Using a browser program like Netscape or Internet Explorer to find out all you want to know about anything you want to know a lot about.

Upload: The opposite of download, when you load something "up" from your computer on to the Internet.

Web page: This is a page that someone has put on the Internet so other computers can get to it, so other people can look at it.

World Wide Web (www): The sort of Internet connecting hookup that makes all this possible.

"So that's what surfing is all about?" I asked, once I started to get a better idea what we were talking about.

"Right!" Yo answered. "So let's do some surfing, okay? What are you interested in?"

"Well, I have this project we're doing for school on the yellow-eyed penguin..."

"Fine! Now we'll just use whatever search engine you like. Shall we try Detect•All?"

"Woah!" I said. "Back the truck up a bit. First of all, what's this Detect•All thing?"

"Sorry. It's a search engine you can use."

"But what's a search engine again?"

"A search engine is a program used by a computer server company to help you find things. When you tell it to find something, it goes through all the things it knows about and checks to see if your search words show up. If it does, it tells you the Internet addresses. All you have to do is click on it and it will download the information from that place or site."

"We better put that in my e-dictionary!" I said, scribbling on my notepad.

Meanwhile things were happening. This is what I saw first of all:

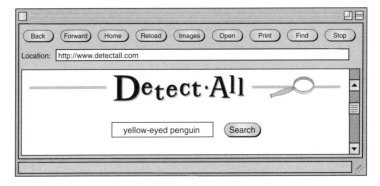

And once I hit the search button next to where I typed "yellow-eyed penguin," I saw:

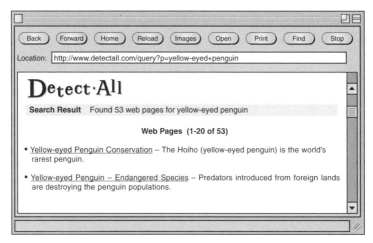

So I clicked on one of the links and then I got:

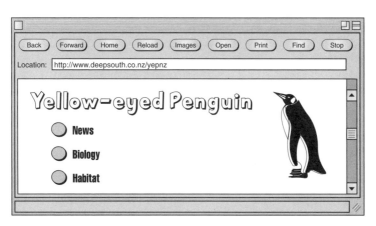

I stared at the screen, "Look at all of this! It's unbelievable! If I had known this was out there, I might have paid a little more attention when I was in computer class."

That was when I remembered Opu's e-mail with the file attached. I asked Yo about that.

"Oh, that's easy," Yo said. "Just click on it."

I clicked on the e-mail attachment. Suddenly the screen filled with a magnificent illustration of a yellow-eyed penguin. Opu had painted it for me!

"Oh, wow! It's fabulous! We'll have to put this on the cover of our report! Look at the color!"

There was a note down at the bottom that said, "I painted this for you. Our computer teacher let

me use her digital camera to photograph it, then she showed me how to send it as an attachment to my message."

"Let's print it out!" I said.

"There's only one hitch," Yo said. "Your printer only prints black and white. You really need a color printer."

At that moment, Dad peeked in my door. "Did I hear that someone needs a color printer?"

"Dad!" I yelled. "You've been listening!"

"No, I haven't," he said, grinning sheepishly. "I was just walking down the hall, and I heard someone say something about a color printer."

"Oh, sure, Dad," I said, grinning back.

"I have very good hearing. I just thought that if you wanted to print something out in color, you could forward the e-mail to my work address and then I could print it out for you."

"E-mail, huh? So, if you weren't listening, how did you know it was an e-mail? Maybe you have x-ray vision, too?" I said, starting to laugh.

Dad didn't know how to answer that one.

But I knew the answer! He'd been snooping! If not, wouldn't he have been more surprised to see me sitting here at the computer? After all the fuss I've made about it, you'd think he would be absolutely amazed! I didn't know whether to be furious with Dad or not, and I couldn't confront him with it because I didn't even know enough yet to ask the right questions.

Worst of all, this had to happen in front of Yo!

That night, Nat kept teasing me and saying things like, "Charlotte has a boyfriend! Charlotte has a boyfriend!"

I tried to ignore him. I sipped soup and nibbled bread and tried to look out the window. But he went on and on. Finally I snapped.

"Listen, pinbrain!" I said. "Yo is in tenth grade, and I'm only in seventh! He's practically old enough to be my mother!"

"Father," Dad said. Then he winced so I knew Mom must have kicked him under the table.

"Boyfriend! Boyfriend!"

"Mom! Will you make him stop?"

"Nat, that's enough now," she said, but she was grinning, too.

"I just want to know when the wedding is!" Noxious Nat said, roaring with laughter.

Mom turned to Nat. "Charlotte's allowed to have a boyfriend if she wants. Leave her alone."

"But he's not my boyfriend! He's just my... my e-friend!"

Chapter 10

The Rain It Raineth Every Day!

Well, New Zealand's version of winter finally arrived. There wasn't a whisker of snow, though. Just cold, rainy days. Every day's weather forecast was the same – either it was going to rain, or it had just finished raining, or it was raining!

Sometimes I didn't mind the rain, especially at night. I'd lie awake and listen to the sound it made on the metal roof. And if there were gusts of wind, it sounded like someone shushing you to sleep. Outside, everything was so green and even though it was winter, there were still quite a few flowers.

The worst part was the cold. Not that it was freezing cold like in Boston, but New Zealand houses and stores were pretty darn chilly. No one had central heating. Instead of heating the whole house, people just heated whatever room they happened to be in at the time. There was only one word for it – weird!

Nat started calling me a "sook." That's a word I heard a lot. A "sook" is someone who complains a lot about anything, and it is definitely not a compliment.

Anyway, it was just like Nat to start calling me that. He was always trying to talk like his New Zealand friends. They'd say things like "G'day" and "Not to worry" and "Ta," so Nat had to imitate them and talk like that, too. I told Mom he was turning into a clone, and she said it was just adolescence. She makes it sound as if adolescence is some sort of disease, and that being a goof is one of the symptoms!

Once it was winter, Nat started playing rugby on Saturdays with kids from his school. He'd trot onto the field, wearing his rugby sweatshirt (only they call it a jersey) and his rugby boots. Then the players would kick a big fat football around and run after it. If anyone was foolish enough to pick it up, the others grabbed him and dragged him onto the ground, and then all the others climbed on top and pushed and shoved and kicked! When he'd come home from playing, he was always covered with mud from head to toe. Does that sound like fun?

To be fair though, Nat was definitely growing less and less nerdy. He actually showed me how to play some pretty cool computer games, and I even managed to beat him a few times, although he said

he let me beat him. My natural response to that, of course, was that I let him let me beat him! That's usually when Mom said something like, "Will you two please stop bickering?"

One winter Sunday, Dad took us down to the waterfront, so we could rent bikes and ride on a gorgeous bike path around the bays that the sea has scooped out of the harbor's edge. Between each of the bays, there were rocky outcrops that jutted out into the harbor. It was sort of like riding around the edges of a piece of a jigsaw puzzle. We rented two tandem bikes. Dad and I were on one and Mom and Nat were on the other.

It was a cold, gray day, but when we got to St. Heliers Bay, we stopped and bought ice-cream cones. The tide was way out, so we sat on the empty beach, licking our cones.

Then we took off our tennis shoes and walked out on the mudflats in our bare feet. It was really cold, but we didn't mind. It was funny to feel the soft, silty harbor mud oozing up between my toes. I looked at my feet. They seemed to be getting bigger and bigger! Just like the rest of me. Ever since I'd arrived in New Zealand, I seemed to have hit some major growth spurt. They really weren't going to recognize me back in the States.

July the fourth was approaching fast. That was the day we were scheduled to head back to Boston. My American friends started to get pretty excited. They kept saying they were planning all kinds of celebrations for my arrival! Sometimes I received as many as ten e-mails a night from them! In a way, I felt really excited about going home again, but I felt strange about leaving my New Zealand friends, too. Much to my surprise, I realized how much I was going to miss all of them. I couldn't win! There was no way I could be in two places at once – why had my parents done this to me?

One Saturday, about a month before we were supposed to go home again, I was feeling torn between the two countries. It was raining so hard that Nat's rugby game was canceled. He and I were playing Monopoly – only it was the computer version. It wasn't quite as good as having the real money to count, but it was okay.

"You know, there is a way you can be in two places at once," Nat was telling me, in response to my tale of woe.

"It's not possible," I said. "Unless you're in some kind of science fiction story!"

"Don't be so technical about it. But what if you had your own web page? Then you could let your friends know what you were doing, no matter where they are or where you are."

"A web page?"

Nat began to laugh. "In fact, you could call it Charlotte's Web Page – like the book!"

"Please don't start calling me a spider again," I warned. When I was younger, he used to tease me because I'm named Charlotte and my absolute favorite book was *Charlotte's Web*.

"No, I'm actually being serious – you really could make your own web page, you know."

"But isn't that hard? Don't you have to know all about – what is it called – that HTML stuff?" I asked suspiciously.

"Not for a simple web page. I've got a program that helps you put it together. You could even scan in some pictures of yourself and have those on your page, too."

"Do you think so?" I asked.

"Why not? I could help you, if you like..."

For the next two or three hours, Nat and I sat at the computer and worked on the web page.

It really didn't say much, just who's page it was and why I had started it. We left a space where I could put a photograph. Nat also showed me how to include a mail to address so people could send me e-mails.

In the end this is what it looked like:

Welcome to Charlotte's Web Page.

I'm Charlotte
and this is me.

If you want to send me an e-mail, you'll make my day.
My e-mail address is:
charlotte@shortland.com
Bye for now!
Charlotte

"Well that's not bad for a start," Nat said.

"But how does it work? How do people get this from my computer to their computer? I'm not going to have all these people visiting my computer, am I?"

"Nah!" Nat laughed. "They don't access your computer, they access your server company's computer."

"Who is this server company?" I asked.

"That's the computer your computer dials when you want to get on the Internet."

"But how do I get my web page onto the server's computer?"

"You send it to them – you upload it."

"But what if I want to change it?"

"That's easy, too. You download it back onto your computer and change it and then send it back to them."

On the Monday after I made my web page, I took a disposable camera with me to school to take photos of all my new friends. Mrs. Caulfield let me photograph in class, too. She even took a photo of me with Ngaire and Emma and Jenny, who I hang around with at school.

And when I got the photos developed, I scanned them in for my web page!

Chapter 11

One Adventure Ends, Another Begins

I couldn't believe it. It was our last week in Auckland. On Saturday night, I slept over at Ngaire's place. Emma and Jenny slept over, too, for a last-night-together "uncelebration."

Emma and Jenny and I slept on a blow-up bed on the floor of Ngaire's bedroom. First we had to pump it up, which was a major piece of engineering! In the night it seemed to go down again so we had to do some more pumping. (Or maybe it went down because we did all kinds of flips and gymnastics on it earlier in the evening!)

Jenny didn't like the dark so we decided to sleep with the light on. But of course, we didn't sleep for ages. Instead we talked. After a while Emma asked if anyone had ever played True Confessions.

"What's that?" we all asked.

"We played it at camp last summer," Emma said. "Everyone has to write a question on a piece

of paper and put it into a hat. It can be any sort of question. You can ask, 'What's your favorite color?' or 'Who's your favorite movie star?' or 'Who do you like?' or anything. Then we sit in a circle, and we have a bottle that someone spins. When it stops, whoever it points to has to take a question out of the hat and answer it absolutely truthfully!"

"What happens if you don't?" I asked.

"I don't know... you get struck by lightning?!" Emma said after a second.

We all laughed.

"Shall we play it?" Ngaire asked.

I thought it sounded a little silly, but I didn't want to be the person that said so, so I said okay. So did everyone else.

"Spin the bottle!" Emma said.

Jenny gave the bottle a hard turn. After two or three spins it came to rest pointing at Jenny. She read the question she chose, then started to rock back and forth in a fit of giggles.

"What is it?"

"Hurry up!"

"We haven't got all night!"

"Yes, we have!"

Jenny managed to squelch her giggles. She cleared her throat, and read, "Have you ever kissed a boy?"

"True confessions, remember?"

"What's the answer?"

"Have you kissed a boy?"

"Of course I have!" said Jenny.

We all screamed and rolled our eyes.

"Who?"

"My little brother, of course!"

We all groaned with disappointment.

On the next spin, the bottle pointed at Emma. She reached into the hat and pulled out a piece of paper. She looked at it and wrinkled her nose.

"What does it say?" asked Ngaire.

Emma frowned and read, "Who would you like to go to the movies with?"

We all began to laugh.

"True confession!"

"You have to tell!"

"Who? Who? Who?"

"I like to go to the movies with... with...."

"The suspense is killing us!"

"My dad, because he always buys us lots of popcorn!"

"Cop-out!" we cried. "Time for a new game."

Two days later we stuffed our lives back in suitcases again. We said good-bye to lots of people again. We climbed into a taxi and drove to an airport again. And we were belted into our airplane seats again. I even got the window seat again. We flew out in the early evening. It had been raining most of the day. Ngaire, Emma, and Jenny came by in the morning with a present for me. It was in a big brown paper bag. They hadn't wrapped it because they said you only did that for parties and my going wasn't a party. I opened the bag. Inside was a stuffed animal – a life-sized yellow-eyed penguin. I decided it had to go with me in my carry-on bag. Mom said there wasn't enough room for another thing, but I managed to scrunch everything up and squeeze it in. I knew when I got back to Boston, it was going to sit on my bed with my other stuffed animals – a friendly reminder of Down Under.

No one had wanted to talk in the taxi out to the airport. The taxi driver told us to make sure we had our tickets and passports. Then the driver tried to cheer us up by talking about the weather.

"We could do with a bit of sunshine," he said.

No one replied.

"Guess you'll be glad to be back home again, then?" the driver asked.

Dad nodded "yes," but just to be polite.

The taxi driver gave up on us and fell silent.

I looked out the window and watched the ground crew loading the luggage. I could hear them from inside the plane, moving things around underneath our feet. The sound system was playing some boring music. Then, as happens so often in this country, the sky began to change. The clouds parted and a lukewarm sun came seeping through, making the wet concrete gleam. The flight attendants closed the plane doors, there was a lurch, and the plane began to push back. We were on our way once again.

The plane lumbered down the runway, gathering speed. The nose lifted and we were off. We flew out across the Manukau Harbor to the west, and then doubled back across the city. I had my forehead against the glass. Nat leaned forward, too.

"Take a look," I said.

"Thanks."

He leaned in front of me and peered down.

"I can see where we played rugby!" he said. "Well, I think that was it. There are so many green fields..."

Nat sighed. He didn't say anything else. He just sat back in his seat and pretended to look at the magazine on his lap. Nerdy Nat was sad, too! Amazing!

I looked out the window again. We were leaving the city behind and flying across fan-shaped beaches as we headed out across the Pacific Ocean.

I loosened my seat belt so I could turn around and see what my parents were doing in the seats behind us. Believe it or not, my mother had my father's laptop out! She was looking at some book about computers, and she was obviously trying to apply what it said to the computer on the tray in front of her.

What was happening to the world? First Charlotte the Stubborn fell for computers, and

then poor old Mom got sucked in! (Somehow I didn't really mind. I decided I'd give her a hand when we got back to Boston.)

I was going to say something to her, but then I noticed what my father was doing. He had his head against the window, peering out at the city slipping away behind us now. I wasn't sure, but I thought I could actually see tears in his eyes...

Back | Forward | Home | Reload | Images

Location: http://www.charlotteswebpage.com

Welcome to

Charlotte's

Web Page

This is an invitation to all my fabulous friends in Boston and to all my fabulous friends in Auckland, NZ. For those who live in the U.S., New Zealand is the two little islands that almost fall off the side of your map on the bottom right-hand side!)

Anyway, you are all invited to an e-mail party right here on my web page (naturally, that's Charlotte's Web Page!).

Everyone has to bring a joke, and we're going to play some real time* e-mail games! Like "E-mail Consequences" and "E-mail Fictionary" and "E-mail Never-Ending Stories" and "E-mail Toppers."

(*If you want to know what "real time" means, you'll need to look it up in my **e-mail dictionary** – or start your own!)

I also want photographs from everyone so I can scan them and put them on my web page so my U.S. friends can get to know my NZ friends and my NZ friends can get to know my U.S. friends.

Hoping to hear from you soon.

Your friend,

Charlotte

From the Author

When I was growing up, my family moved around a lot, from one small New Zealand town to another. Every time we moved, it meant we had to say good-bye to our old friends and make new ones. I guess I can sympathize with Charlotte, because moving to a new place or doing something you've never done before (like learning to use a computer) can be scary at first.

Computers pop up a lot in this story, too. Now I know that computers are only dumb old machines, but I've become rather attached to my machine. I'm also an e-mail fanatic. The first thing I do every morning and the last thing I do every night is check my e-mails. So if you want to send me an e-mail, please feel free – my address is alantc@ihug.co.nz.

Alan Trussell-Cullen

From the Illustrator

I've worked as an editorial artist at The Modesto Bee, a newspaper in Modesto, California, for sixteen years. Right now, I'm living in Denver, Colorado, for a year to fulfill my dream of illustrating children's books. It's wonderful to see my artwork in the newspaper everyday, but to see it in a book that will be kept for more than a day is incredible!

I'd like to thank The Bee for granting me the time to take on this project, and my children, Leslie and Russell, and my sister, Janice, for their support and understanding.

I can identify with how Charlotte uses e-mail to keep in touch with her friends back home – I use it to keep in touch with my friends, too!

Lauren McAdam

© Text by **Alan Trussell-Cullen**
Illustrated by **Lauren McAdam**
Edited by **Rebecca McEwen**
Designed by **Karen Baxa Hoglund**

05 04 03 02 01
10 9 8 7 6 5 4 3

Distributed in the United States of America by
    Rigby
    a division of Reed Elsevier Inc.
    1000 Hart Road
    Barrington, IL 60010

Printed in China
ISBN: 0-7699-0410-6